ISBN 0-86163-105-6
© AWARD PUBLICATIONS LIMITED 1981
Spring House, Spring Place
LONDON NW5, England
Printed in Belgium
Reprinted 1984

The Pied Piper of Hamelin

Stories retold by Kay Brown

Illustrated by Gerry Embleton

The town of Hamelin in Northern Germany is famous today because of something which happened there hundreds of years ago. The city is on the banks of the River Weser and was, even then, a large, busy place with many fine buildings.

But Hamelin was a terrible place to live, for one reason –RATS!!

The town was overrun by huge, fearless rats: they attacked the dogs and cats and bit the children in their beds. These rats didn't hide until darkness fell before they searched for food. Oh no, these rats swarmed everywhere all day long, jumped onto tables, and gnawed at the food in the kitchens while it was being cooked! The noise of their squeaking and screaming filled the streets, but whatever the people of Hamelin tried to do to get rid of the rats seemed to have no effect.

At last the townspeople could stand it no longer. They stormed into the Town Hall and confronted the Mayor. "What are you doing about the rats?" they shouted angrily. "Or do you spend all day sitting in fine clothes eating fine lunches – which *we* pay for – while the rest of us suffer? Something *must* be done!"

The Mayor and Councillors were not a little afraid of the shouting crowds and certainly didn't want to lose their fur-trimmed robes of office or the seven-course dinners they enjoyed from time to time! "Surely someone can think of something," wailed the Mayor. "Let's send the town-crier into every square in the city to ask for good ideas, offer a reward perhaps . . . " So the very next day a messenger was heard in every part of Hamelin reading the Mayor's proposal to the crowds:
"THERE WILL BE A REWARD OF ONE THOUSAND GOLD COINS FOR WHOEVER CAN RID THE TOWN OF ITS PLAGUE OF RATS."

Well, of course everyone *had* been trying to think of a way to get rid of the rats, but they tried even harder on hearing about the reward. Engineers designed huge traps to catch the pests; chemists sat up all night trying to find a poison strong enough to kill them without killing all the

people too. Hunters talked about organising an army to shoot them one by one – and someone even suggested that everyone should leave the city and let the rats stay! But no one, it seemed, had an idea which would work.

With every day that passed the rats seemed to grow in size and number, and the people grew more desperate.

One morning, during a Council meeting, the doors burst open and there stood a tall, thin stranger. He was dressed in most peculiar clothes of brightest red and yellow; his tunic had long draped sleeves, there was a jaunty feather in his wide-brimmed hat and around his neck on a long cord was a strange pipe.

He smiled mysteriously at the startled Mayor.

In a soft voice, and very politely, he said, "Your honours, I have come halfway round the world to solve your problem. I have been of service to Kings in the West and Sultans in the East and by means of a secret charm I am here in Hamelin to rid you of your rats and claim the reward!"

The Mayor and all the Councillors welcomed him warmly – it seemed as though their prayers had been answered at last. Promising him whatever he wished they urged the stranger to begin his magic at once.

He stepped out into the street and raised the strange pipe to his lips. With eyes twinkling the piper played three high-pitched notes and waited. Far away there was a muttering, mumbling sound; gradually it grew louder like thunder rolling in from the hills. Suddenly, from every house and hole, from every shop and cellar, the rats appeared – old rats, young rats, big rats, small rats, rats of every colour and description. Whatever magic was in the piper's call, the rats were following him as though their lives depended on it.

Through the narrow streets and across the squares the piper danced, playing his shrill notes – and the little creatures followed. More joined the throng at every corner, until it seemed the cobbles were alive with a squealing sea of rats. The townspeople stared from their windows – they couldn't believe what they saw! Who was the prancing stranger dressed in such odd and colourful clothes? What was the magic of his music that no rat could ignore it, but was compelled to scramble and scurry after him across the streets of Hamelin?

On and on the piper sped, right across the city, never tiring, until dusk was falling and he came to the banks of the River Weser.

But the piper played on, wading into the dark water. After him came the rats! They rushed to the river's edge and desperately, blindly, hurled themselves after the stranger. For several hours more the pipe was heard and well into the night the splashing and squealing continued . . . until, at last, every rat was drowned.

Next day, when the people of Hamelin realised
that the rats had really gone, there was rejoicing in
every part of the town. Free from the pests which had
plagued their lives, night and day, for as long as anyone
could remember! Men, women and children danced and
sang in the streets. There was feasting and music and
laughter everywhere. "Hurrah for the piper, the Pied Piper
of Hamelin!" the happy people cried.

But in the Town Hall, where the piper had gone to collect his money, no one appeared at all grateful.

Having watched the rats drowning in the river the night before, the Mayor felt quite safe in paying the piper not more than one gold coin – instead of the thousand he had promised.

The stranger listened in silence to the Mayor, then his face darkened and he shook with anger. Saying not one word he raced from the room, up the stone steps and onto the roof of the Town Hall. As he stood angrily shaking his fists over the city the skies clouded over and a cold wind began to blow.

The piper stepped down into the street and once more lifted his pipe to his lips. He blew three long, clear notes – then waited and listened.

Faces appeared at doors and windows; women stopped their chattering and men straightened from their work. What was the stranger doing now? Why was he still playing his magic pipe now that all the rats were gone?

Then the children, in two's and three's, came out from their houses, laughing and chattering. At first they came slowly, as if they weren't sure where they were going or why, but the piper began his music again and moved off down the street. Little feet began to run, more children came to join the first, clapping their hands and skipping. When the piper turned the corner the children followed, and the sound of their happy laughter mingled with the music.

As he had done the day before, the piper danced and played his way across Hamelin, through every lane and across every square. Everywhere he passed his sweet music brought out more children to join the chattering crowd at his heels: they joined hands and ran after him without once looking back.

They passed the Town Hall once more, where the Mayor and Councillors stood dumbstruck, unable to move or cry out, and on by the old cathedral at the edge of the city.

By now hundreds were following the piper – every child who was old enough to walk was there – and all were with him as he turned towards the River Weser where the rats had perished.

Just as the horrified
onlookers felt sure their children
were going to drown as the rats had
done, the piper turned to the West, towards a great hill which
looked down on Hamelin. "Thank goodness," the people thought
with great relief, "they'll never be able to cross Koppelberg Hill.
The piper will have to stop, and our children too."

But, as they watched, unbelievably the side of the hill seemed to open: a narrow, dark corridor appeared and the piper, followed by the children, disappeared inside. When all were gone the great door shut fast and there was silence.

Only one child was left, a lame boy who hadn't been able to keep up with his friends.

As you may imagine, the town of Hamelin was a very sad and quiet place for many years afterwards, and the story of that awful day was carved on a stone by the Koppelberg Hill – as a reminder to all that a promise, once made, should be kept.

Beauty and The Beast

There was once a merchant who, because of bad luck and greedy partners, had lost almost all his money. His wife was dead, but he had three daughters who had been used to the best of everything all their lives. One day, quite suddenly, they were told by their father to pack a few belongings as they were to move to a tiny cottage in the country.

When the girls saw their new home the two oldest – who were rather spoiled – began complaining that they could never be happy in such a poor house. The youngest daughter, however, whose kind heart and ready smile had earned her the name of Beauty, took their father's hand. Trying to comfort him, she said, "It may not be very grand, but at least here we may all stay together."

After almost a year in their new home
the merchant heard some good news: a ship
bringing goods for him to sell was due in
harbour. He decided to journey there at once!
After all those months with no luxuries or
presents you can imagine how excited the
girls were! The eldest daughter asked her
father to bring back a fine silk gown,
trimmed with lace, in a colour to match her

hair. The second girl wanted a fur bonnet
from the most expensive shop in town.
Laughing, their father promised to do his
best. "But Beauty," he asked. "What shall I
bring for you?" All she really wanted was her
father's safe return, but in case she made her
sisters seem greedy by asking for nothing for
herself, Beauty said, "I miss the flowers in
our old garden: please bring me a rose."

But the merchant's good luck didn't last. When, after travelling for two days, he arrived at the docks he was told that the ship had sunk in a storm and all her cargo had been lost.

Sadly he turned for home. As night fell, cold and exhausted, he became hopelessly lost in a snowstorm. His horse stumbled on against the icy wind until it seemed he could go no further. Just as the merchant was wondering whether he would ever see his family again he glimpsed, through the swirling snow, the glowing lights of a distant castle.

It was the strangest castle he had ever seen!
Falling from his horse he stumbled up the
steps—and found the huge door open!

Although he was by now rather frightened, Beauty's father was so tired and cold that he forgot his fear and went inside.

He called "Hello – is anyone here?" as he walked across the great hall, but heard only the moan of the wind and the echo of his own voice. But how could the castle be deserted, he wondered, when the shadows of crackling wood-fires and lighted candles danced in every room?

At last, too weak to care, he found a warm bed and fell into it gratefully.

When he awoke early next morning he couldn't find his own threadbare clothes – but in their place was a velvet suit, fur-trimmed cloak and leather boots, all of which fitted the astonished merchant perfectly! There was a further surprise downstairs, for although dawn had not yet broken a freshly-prepared breakfast awaited him!

Having slept and eaten well, the merchant left the strange castle to find his horse and continue his journey. As he crossed the snow-covered garden he saw a single rose-bush in bloom and, remembering Beauty's request, plucked one of the flowers.

Instantly he heard a voice behind him roar, "Have I not given you enough, that you must steal the flowers from my garden?" He turned and was terrified to see a huge, hairy shape in a man's cloak, but with the claws and teeth of a beast!

"For your greed you must send me the first living thing which greets you on your return home!" it bellowed.

The merchant ran to his horse and rode as fast as he could until well out of sight of the castle. As he travelled he thought about the Beast's demand and hoped fervently that his dog or one of the hens might be the first creature he saw. But, as he had feared, it was Beauty who ran to welcome him, for she had been watching the lane for his return.

Miserably her father told of his bad luck in town, of finding the strange castle and of his terrible promise to the Beast. Beauty couldn't bear to see her father so troubled. She tried to appear cheerful as she packed her few possessions and said goodbye to him and her sisters, but none of them knew if they would ever meet again.

Reaching the mysterious
castle Beauty found, as her
father had, that everything
had been thought of to make
her comfortable. But there
was no sign of the Beast,
although Beauty often sensed
a lonely figure watching her
from the shadows.

One morning Beauty came down to breakfast to find the Beast waiting for her. She stopped on the stairs, terrified by his strange appearance, but he spoke in a gruff, gentle voice. "Please Beauty, do not be afraid. I shall never harm you."

Beauty and the Beast shared one
meal every day after that, but
although Beauty tried to talk to
him the Beast spoke very little and
kept his face turned away.

After a few weeks Beauty found
herself looking forward to their
meetings and to the rose he
remembered to leave for her
each day.

Many months passed and Beauty grew to know the huge castle and its lovely gardens. Early one misty morning, in her favourite part of the garden, she was surprised to see the Beast shuffling towards her. He knelt at her feet and asked her quietly in his rough voice, "Beauty, are you fond of me?" "Of course, dear kind Beast," she replied. "Beauty… will you marry me?" he whispered. Beauty was shocked by the sudden question, but didn't wish to hurt the gentle creature. "No," she replied. "I couldn't marry you – but I hope we may still be friends?"

The Beast said nothing; his great head hung low on his chest and he wandered slowly away.

The next day, in a magic mirror on her bedroom wall, Beauty saw her father, grey and thin, calling to her from his sick-bed. She was horrified to see how old and worried he looked; if only she could talk to him, tell him she was safe and well…

At dinner that evening Beauty begged the Beast to allow her to visit her father, promising to return as soon as he was well. The Beast sadly agreed, but gave Beauty a magic ring with which to signal her readiness to return to the castle.

Beauty awoke next morning to find herself outside her father's cottage!

The old man was overjoyed to see her again and immediately began to feel better. Even Beauty's sisters seemed glad she was safely home and they all listened in amazement to her stories of the Beast and his castle.

Beauty quickly settled down with her family again; her father's health improved every day now that his dearest daughter was home. The weeks passed happily – and Beauty forgot her promise to the Beast.

Alone once more, the sad Beast wandered through his gardens at night howling for Beauty. With each day that passed he grew more unhappy; he could neither eat nor sleep.

One evening, as Beauty prepared supper for her father and sisters, she felt the chill light of the moon through the cottage window. The magic ring which the Beast had given her seemed to flash urgently. Suddenly Beauty remembered her promise and realised she had left her kind friend to die!

Horrified at her own heartlessness, Beauty rushed to her waiting horse and returned to the castle. She ran from room to room, searching and calling, without success; at last she found the Beast lying under a tree. His eyes were closed and his great paws cold and still.

"Beauty… Beauty… you have come back," he whispered, turning his head away as if to hide. "Please… don't look at me… I'm so ugly…" Beauty was heartbroken.

"Dear Beast," she cried, taking a paw
to warm it in her small hands. "Dear,
wonderful Beast! Please don't die – I love
you," and her tears fell onto his rough fur.

When Beauty next opened her tear-filled eyes she couldn't believe what she saw: gone were the claws and fur of the Beast, and instead her hands held those of a young man!

Smiling lovingly, he explained that a wicked fairy had long ago used her evil magic to change him from a royal prince into a beast; the spell could only be broken if a kind and honest girl came freely to love him – as Beauty had!

The very next week Beauty and her prince were married: her father and sisters came to live in the strange castle, and all lived very happily ever after.

Ali Baba and the Forty Thieves

from Stories of the Arabian Nights

Ali Baba was a poor woodcutter in a small town in Persia. His brother, Cassim, had married a rich wife and lived a life of ease, but Ali Baba had to work hard to earn his living. Just the same, he was cheerful and well-liked.

While Ali Baba was cutting wood one day he heard the sound of many horses nearby. As everyone knew there to be a fierce band of robbers in the area Ali Baba hid his donkeys and climbed a tree for safety. He was just in time, for they were indeed robbers, and they stopped near the very spot where Ali Baba was hiding.

The men waited while their leader dismounted and, having looked about him (but fortunately not above him!), strode over to a large rock. Raising his arms, he said loudly *"Open Sesame!"* To Ali Baba's astonishment the wall of the rock split open and the robbers disappeared inside carrying their saddlebags. The door shut after the last man and remained closed for some time, but Ali Baba dared not climb down from his uncomfortable hiding place. Just as he was wondering whether to stretch his legs he saw the robbers emerge from the rock: this time Ali Baba counted them – there were forty including the captain – and noticed that the saddlebags were now empty.

When all the men had ridden away Ali Baba jumped down and examined the rock, which appeared quite solid. Remembering the captain's words he shouted *"Open Sesame!"*

It worked! The door rumbled open and Ali Baba, rather hesitantly, stepped inside into the darkness.

But dark though it was, he could see shining and sparkling in the cave such treasure as he had never imagined – chests of diamonds, coffers of gold coins, silver jugs and jewelled swords! So this was where the forty thieves had hidden their spoils.

It didn't take Ali Baba long to realise he could now be a rich man like his brother. Worried in case the robbers returned, he quickly caught his donkeys, emptied the wood-baskets and half filled them with gold, which he covered with logs. He ordered the cave to close as the captain had done, then hurried home to tell his wife the wonderful news.

She, too, was amazed at his good luck, but was worried that the robbers might come after her husband to get back the gold! She persuaded Ali Baba to count it, then hide it in the garden and use only a little at a time so no-one would be suspicious of their sudden wealth.

But there were far too many coins to count, so Ali Baba
suggested they borrow his brother's measure to save time.

When Cassim's wife agreed to lend the measure she couldn't
help wondering why her brother-in-law should need it, for
everyone knew how poor he was. Out of curiosity she fixed a
small piece of wax to the bottom of the measure.

When the measure was returned, Cassim and his wife were astonished to see a solid gold coin stuck to the wax.

"How can it be that my woodcutter brother, who has never had two brass coins to rub together, now has so many of these gold pieces that he must borrow a measure to count them?" wondered the jealous Cassim. "I must follow him tomorrow and find out what my dear brother does when he's supposed to be cutting wood!"

This he did, unknown to Ali Baba–who led him to the robbers' cave.

From his hiding place Cassim watched, and heard his brother speak the magic words *"Open Sesame!"* Then he saw the rock part and Ali Baba step inside. Almost too excited to keep quiet, Cassim waited for his brother to re-appear: when he did so he was carrying several leather bags which Cassim felt sure contained more gold coins. Ali Baba ordered the door to close, loaded his donkeys as before, and set off into the forest the way he had come

Out of hiding Cassim ran to the rock and, remembering what Ali Baba had said, shouted *"Open Sesame!"* Sure enough the magic worked for him, too, and in the dark cave he found the thieves' hidden treasure. "Wonderful! Marvellous!" shrieked the greedy Cassim (who was already quite rich enough); he raced from gold to silver, from diamonds to emeralds, filling as many bags as he could.

But this took some time and Cassim's mind was so full
of how he would spend his new wealth that, when at last he
was ready to leave the cave, he couldn't remember the magic
words to open the door! *"Open Sizzle!"* he tried; when
this failed he tried again: *"Open Saveloy!"* and then, in
desperation, *"Open Sausage!"* But the door, of course,
remained shut fast!

Later that day, as they always did, the robbers returned to their cave. As the door opened at the captain's command out rushed Cassim – straight into the arms of the thieves, who killed him instantly. They were puzzled to know how anyone else could have discovered a way into the secret cave and, in case Cassim had not been alone, the captain ordered his body to be cut into four pieces and left just inside the cave door as a warning. This was done.

When Cassim hadn't returned that evening his wife was so worried she went to Ali Baba and confessed that they had found out about the gold. She told him how Cassim had set out to follow Ali Baba that morning and hadn't come home again.

Ali Baba offered to search for Cassim, but he felt sure the robbers must have discovered his brother; when he opened the door to the cave he saw he had been right. Although he was very upset, Ali Baba had to work quickly in case the thieves returned and caught him, too. He loaded his brother's body onto the donkeys and hurried home in the dark.

He broke the terrible news to Cassim's wife and told her how important it was the robbers didn't find out that he, too, knew the secret of the cave. For safety he asked their faithful servant, Morgiana, to find someone reliable who could sew Cassim's body together before he was buried so that everyone would think he had died naturally. Morgiana knew an old shoe-mender nearby who was short-sighted but very trustworthy, and she offered him a piece of the gold if he would do as she asked. Baba Mustapha, for that was the old man's name, agreed and that night was led blindfolded to Cassim's house where he did as he had promised.

Meanwhile, the captain of the robbers had returned to the cave: he was amazed to find that Cassim's body had been removed. "Now I'm sure there must be more than one who knows our secret," he thought. "Somehow I must find him and silence him forever."

As he didn't hear gossip in the next few days about any unusual deaths in the town he realised the parts of Cassim's body must have been sewn together before the funeral. He therefore went quietly to the tailor, the dress-maker and, lastly, to the shoe-mender to ask, in a roundabout way, if they had done any sewing recently that was different and secret. At first Baba Mustapha wouldn't talk, but he was poor and two gold pieces eventually loosened his tongue; he agree to be blindfolded once more and to try and find the house to which he had been led.

That evening, when most people were eating their supper, the robber captain and Baba Mustapha made their way slowly through the streets of the town. "Ah yes," said Baba Mustapha suddenly. "This is the way — I remember how uneven the path was just here." He stopped outside Cassim's house, where Ali Baba and his wife now also lived. "This . . . yes, this is the very house!" The thief was delighted (and very pleased with his own cleverness!); he thanked Baba Mustapha and paid him the promised gold piece. So that he would remember the house he marked the door with a large cross, then crept away to fetch his men.

Luckily, however, Morgiana had been out to borrow some salt and she returned just after the robber captain had left. She saw the painted cross on the door, but couldn't think of the reason for it. Being very cunning (and remembering what had recently happened to Cassim) she marked several other doors in the street in the same way.

In the middle of the night, when everyone else was asleep, the robber captain returned with his band of men. "This is the house," he said proudly. "I know because I marked the door with this cross." Imagine his fury when the robbers pointed out crosses on the doors of the other houses each side!

There was nothing they could do but creep back to the forest and think of another plan to trap Ali Baba.

The robber captain was now even more determined to find the man who knew the secret of the cave, and he swore not to rest until they had caught and killed him.

He went back to Baba Mustapha and, with a promise of four gold pieces this time, was again led to the house where Ali Baba was now living. But this time the captain took no chances: he examined the front of the house so carefully that there could be no second mistake.

Returning to his band of men, who were awaiting their orders in the forest hideout, he told them of his plan to get into Ali Baba's house. They were to hide inside some empty oil jars slung over the backs of a team of donkeys: only one jar was to be full of oil, to fool Ali Baba if he became suspicious. Then, pretending to be a weary oil merchant, the robber captain made his way to Ali Baba's house, to ask for lodgings for the night.

Ali Baba was pleased to help a tired traveller (for he didn't recognise the captain in his disguise). Later that evening, before he went to bed, the captain crept into the courtyard where the donkeys were tied and carefully lifted the jars to the ground, telling each robber inside that he would tap on his jar when the time came to attack.

Morgiana, Ali Baba's servant, was in the kitchen preparing the next day's meals, when her lamp dimmed and went out. "No oil in the lamp and none in the cupboard," she said crossly to herself "What shall I do? But wait, there's plenty in the merchant's jars – I'll use some of that tonight and the master can pay him for it tomorrow."

But when she tapped the first jar to see if it was full of oil the robber within, thinking that it

was his captain's signal, answered "Ready, sir."
Morgiana soon realised what was happening when
she went from that jar to the next, and the next, and
heard the same words from every hidden robber.
Finding the real jar of oil at last she took it back to the
kitchen and heated it on the fire until the oil boiled.
She then carefully poured a measure of boiling oil into
each robber's jar! Then she hid in the shadows to see
what would happen next.

Scarcely ten minutes later she heard the captain of the robbers creep down into the courtyard. Hearing no answer from the first jar he tapped, he peered inside... He could scarcely believe what he found in that jar, and in all the others!

Now he was alone. He cursed Ali Baba and swore he would spend the rest of his life, if necessary, getting even with him. He returned to the forest, and so determined and angry was he that another plan had taken shape before the night was over.

He went back to the city next morning and, by midday, had found what he was looking for – an empty shop in the market place. Pretending to be a shopkeeper, he spread out before him some clothes and pots, then sat down to wait for Ali Baba – for he knew that everyone in the town came to market at some time.

Sure enough, after a few days, he saw Ali Baba stop at a nearby stall; he spent a long time talking to the young man who ran the stall without buying anything.

When Ali Baba had left, the robber stopped the young man
and began to chat to him in a friendly way. He soon learned
that this was Ali Baba's son and that Ali Baba came often to

talk to him in the market square. The cunning thief was very charming and Ali Baba's son was as good-natured and trusting as his father: soon he believed he had found a new friend.

When his father next came to see him, Ali Baba's son introduced him to his new friend. For a second time Ali Baba didn't recognise the robber and shook his hand warmly. "My son has few friends," he said. "We should be honoured if you will be our guest at dinner this evening." The robber, of course, accepted readily: this was exactly what he had been hoping for.

However, when he arrived at the house that evening, clever Morgiana saw through the robber's disguise and was sure why he had come. While the men were drinking their wine and talking before the meal Morgiana disguised herself as a dancer, with veiled head-dress and satin belt. Into the wide belt she slipped a silver dagger.

As Morgiana danced the music grew faster and faster: she whirled around the room with veils flying – and stopped... in front of the disguised robber. In a flash she drew the dagger from her belt and plunged it deep into his chest, while Ali Baba and his son looked on in amazement.

Of course, once Morgiana had explained who the merchant was and why he had come, Ali Baba couldn't thank her enough. "You saved my life three times. What can I give you?" he asked. "Anything I have is yours!" "Let me have my freedom," answered the servant. "That is what I most wish for."

Very soon there was a wedding in the family, for Ali Baba's son and Morgiana had loved one another for a long time and, now she was no longer a servant, they were able to marry.

So Ali Baba lived for many, many years, enjoying the treasure he had found in the robbers' cave.